A Flat in Paris

BY GUILLAUME MUSSO

BOOK ANALYSIS

Written by Marianne Coche
Translated by Oliver Brown

A Flat in Paris

BY GUILLAUME MUSSO

GUILLAUME MUSSO

FRENCH WRITER

- **Born in 1974 in Antibes**
- **Some of his works:**
    - *And After...* (2004), novel
    - *The Paper Girl* (2010), novel
    - *The Angel's Call* (2011), novel

Born in 1974 in Antibes, Guillaume Musso became aware of his vocation as a writer very early on. At the age of nineteen, he spent time in New York, which already inspired him to write many ideas for novels. He graduated in economics and taught this subject until 2008. In 2004, his book *Et Après... was published in 2004*, selling one million copies and translated into twenty languages. Readers have continued to be enthusiastic about each of his novels, such as *Sauve-moi* (2005), *Seras-tu là?* (2006), *Parce que je t'aime* (2007), etc. Today he is one of the public's favourite authors and several of his works have been adapted for the cinema.

A FLAT IN PARIS

AN UNEXPECTED THRILLER
WITH A BACKGROUND OF AN INITIATION QUEST

- **Genre**: Thriller

- **Reference edition**: Un Appartement à Paris, Paris, Pocket, 2018, 542 p.

- **1st edition**: 2017

- **Themes**: investigation, love, art, revenge, motherhood

Part thriller, part coming-of-age story, this 2017 novel by Guillaume Musso tells the story of an unexpected encounter between two characters who seem to have nothing in common: Madeline, a former policewoman from London; and Gaspard, a renowned American playwright. Forced to share their Parisian rental apartment following a computer error, the two of them make a discovery about Sean Lorenz, the former owner of the house they are renting, which plunges them into the heart of an unexpected investigation. Multiple twists and turns will lead them from Paris to New York, but also to confront their inner demons.

SUMMARY

PARIS AND THE MISSING PAINTINGS

On Tuesday 20 December, as he does every year, the American playwright Gaspard Coutances arrived at Roissy Charles de Gaulle airport to spend a month in isolation in a Parisian flat writing his new play.

Madeline Greene, a former London policewoman, arrived at the Gare du Nord by Eurostar and rented a holiday home to rebuild her life after a suicide attempt, to regain her strength and to be able to undergo the *in vitro* fertilisation process she has decided to undertake. For her, the procedure is the last chance she has to have a child.

Due to a computer error, Madeline and Gaspard are forced to share the same house: the studio of Sean Lorenz, a former New York graffiti artist who became a famous painter and is now dead.

Upset, Madeline contacts and meets Bernard Benedick, the gallery owner responsible for renting the house he inherited from Sean Lorenz, his former artist friend. By the way she asks questions, Bernard guesses that the young woman belongs to the police and, learning that she has worked on kidnapping and homicide cases, invites her to lunch. In addition to the house, Sean has also left him a matchbox from a restaurant he used to frequent, on which he has inscribed a quotation from Apollinaire: "It's high time to light up the stars again". It is, in fact, a clue left by the painter to reveal the location of his last three paintings, which the gallery owner has been searching for in vain since his friend's death. Bernard Bénédick has a hunch that she will be able to find them, and entrusts Madeline with the mission.

Meanwhile, Gaspard explores the house and discovers a biography of Sean Lorenz which fascinates him. Disturbed by deafening music, the playwright goes to the neighbour's house, Pauline Delatour. In conversation with her, he learns that Lorenz had indeed started to paint again a few days before his death. However, contrary to his daytime habits, the artist only painted at night.

That evening, Madeline and Gaspard share their respective discoveries about Lorenz's life and work over dinner: two years earlier, Béatriz Muñoz, an old friend of Sean's, kidnapped and sequestered his wife Penelope and their son Julian in New York. The kidnapping ended in the death of the little boy, plunging the painter into total confusion and making him return to his demons: alcohol, drugs and medication. Against all odds, he begins to paint again some time before his death, lulled by the mad hope that his son is still alive, thus confirming the existence of the three paintings.

The discovery of all these elements marks Madeline and Gaspard, so much so that they decide to embark on a quest for the paintings, each on their own: they can only stand each other for one meal. Their investigations leac them to meet several people from the painter's entourage: Penelope Kurkowski, his ex-wife; Diane Raphaël, his psychiatrist and friend; and Jean-Michel Fayol, his colour dealer.

It is finally by going to the restaurant where the matchbox came from that Madeline and Gaspard take the first decisive step in their investigation. While examining the mosaic that the painter had placed in this place that he had started to frequent again, they discover a carefully hidden QR code. This code gives access to a quotation from Oscar Wilde, also referring to stars. When Bernard Benedick tells them that little Julian went to the School of the Stars, Madeline and Gaspard go to the site. There, remembering that Gustave Courbet's painting *The Origin of the World* was hidden by another painting, Gaspard cuts out three children's paintings behind which Sean had in fact h dden his final productions. On the last of these, the phrase "Julian is alive" is drawn in phosphorescent paint and repeated across the canvas.

NEW YORK AND LITTLE JULIAN

Convinced that Sean and Penelope's son is dead, Madeline travels to Spain to have her eggs retrieved.

On his side, not satisfied with this outcome, Gaspard pushes his investigations further and, thanks to the documents and objects he discovers in the painter's belongings, allows himself to be persuaded that little

Julian is still alive. However, knowing that these elements will not be enough to convince Madeline, he modifies Sean's telephone records and prints a newspaper article talking about the young policewoman's work where he highlights certain passages, in order to make her believe that it was her that the artist wanted to see during his last stay in New York. In exchange for her promise never to see him again, the young woman agrees to follow Gaspard to the United States.

As soon as they arrive in New York, Gaspard and Madeline regain a taste for life, he because he finds a familiar place, she because she gradually recovers her investigative instincts.

Their respective investigations soon lead them to discover that Adriano Sotomayor, the third member of the Artificiers – the group of graffiti artists to which Sean and Beatriz belonged – is far from the upright policeman he portrayed himself to be. Indeed, the man turns out to be responsible not only for the death of his half-brother, but also for the kidnapping, abduction and murder of several young children. These crimes were part of a machiavellian plan to take revenge on his mother, who had abandoned him to an abusive father when he was only five years old.

When Adriano's bank statements show expenses for large amounts of freeze-dried food and baby products, the two budding investigators are hopeful that they can find Julian alive, even though they have found nothing in the old Sotomayor family home. After yet another argument, Madeline and Gaspard discover that Adriano's father owned a boat, she while looking at a photo and he while talking to a local. It is there that they finally find little Julian, in a critical state, but alive.

While they are on the road to take him to the hospital, Gaspard makes a proposal to Madeline: return the child to the authorities and resume their lives separately, or offer Julian a family. Madeline chooses the latter. They set fire to the boat to get rid of all the evidence and, after having Julian's papers redone, the three of them go to live in Greece, on the island of Snifos, where Gaspard owns a sailboat.

CHARACTER STUDY

MADELINE GREENE

Madeline Greene's life is chaotic. First a member of the Manchester crime squad, which she left following a terrible case (*The Angel's Call*, 2011) that psychologically destroyed her, she then moved to Paris where she became a florist. There, the young woman manages, thanks to a meeting, to take over and solve the investigation which leads her to enter the administrative services of the federal witness protection programme in New York where she ends up as a consultant for closed cases. When she is not satisfied with her job and has no reason to stay in the United States since her boyfriend left her to return to live with his wife and little boy, Madeline quits and returns to England.

Just when she thinks she has healed her wounds, our young heroine ends up attempting suicide after seeing her former partner with his son. It is therefore in order to rebuild herself that, at the end of the year, she arrives in Paris, where she has rented a holiday home and has started an *in vitro* fertilisation procedure. In fact, she sees the time passing by, does not feel capable of loving a man anymore and this intervention seems to be the only possible option to have a child. In reality, as Gaspard Coutances guesses from their first real discussion, this desire for a child is above all aimed at filling a feeling of solitude that she refuses to admit for a long time: "On discovering her image, Madeline was seized by an unexpected spleen. Her loneliness and helplessness appeared to her in all their crudeness" (p. 304). In spite of everything, she shows a form of almost sickly obstinacy in order to satisfy this desire for motherhood, since she imposes on herself the painful process of a preparatory treatment which she can hardly bear and which she wishes to see completed as soon as possible. However, on the other hand, she is unable to visualise her future child.

According to gallery owner Bernard Bénédick, Madeline does not seem to be easy to get along with, a trait that often reappears in her relationships with others. Similarly, when it comes to her personal life, her reactions to the writer and her former friend Takumi, who came to pick her up on her arrival in Paris, show that she is not at peace with herself, despite the confidence she displays. This is reflected in her general appearance, as she still has the same old-fashioned haircut and drags around her old leather jacket.

Even though she is no longer a police officer, the investigations into the paintings of Sean Lorenz and Julian awaken her investigative instincts and gradually bring her back to life: it is 'the spark she has been waiting for all along' (p. 408).

GASPARD COUTANCES

A successful playwright whose plays are performed all over the world, Gaspard Coutances does not have a happy life. "A 'cad, grumpy, shady' (p. 298) and a confirmed bachelor, he leads a well-ordered life: he spends a month cooped up in Paris writing his annual play, six months in the Cyclades where he owns a sailboat and, when the tourist season comes, he leaves Greece for his cottage in Montana. He has no mobile phone or e-mail address and uses Karen, his agent, as an "interface with the outside world. The shield that allowed him to live as he pleased and say fuck it to everyone else." (p. 297-298). Nevertheless, this does not prevent him from intermittently leaving his hermit life to attend one cultural event or another. This ambivalence is reflected in his general appearance, which gives the impression of a man who neglects himself and not the cultured author that he is. "He was a UFO: a sort of misanthropic, pessimistic gentleman, but who, for the duration of a dinner party, could prove a pleasant companion." (p. 123).

He is also a person of integrity who is incapable of lying, but who learns a lot from Madeline.

This surly character can probably be explained by the writer's painful past, marked by the absence of his father caused by his mother, who wanted to deprive him of his parental rights. He also has to deal with his complex relationship with alcohol, of which he is well aware: "Sometimes friend, sometimes foe, alcohol was the shield that kept his emotions at bay, the chain mail that protected him from anxiety, the best of sleeping pills" (p. 54).

SEAN LORENZ

Although this character is dead when the story begins, his shadow is omnipresent throughout the story, which is always based on an element of his life or work.

A former petty criminal who belonged to the Artificiers, a group of New York graffiti artists, Sean Lorenz met and fell in love with a young French woman, Penelope Kurkowski, in 1992. He followed her to Paris where the gallery owner Bernard Bénédick, who was to become his friend, spotted his talent and made him an appreciated painter.

Even though his relationships, both romantic and friendly, are punctuated by ups and downs, Lorenz remains a good person ("He was even rather humble and, although he was obsessed with his painting, this did not prevent him from being interested in people." [p.189]), not hesitating to help his colour dealer financially or to offer a mosaic to the restaurant he liked to frequent. He is the typical example of the tormented artist who loses all his inspiration and desire to paint after the long-awaited birth of his son Julian, a source of immense happiness for him. His austere appearance is transformed in the presence of his child. After the disappearance of the little boy, the painter remains deeply convinced that he is still alive, and this hope rekindles his artistic flame.

THE OTHER CHARACTERS

Bernard Bénédick

It was the gallery owner who spotted Sean Lorenz's talent when he arrived in Paris, before becoming his friend and the godfather of little Julian. He is the legatee of the artist's property and house, and it is he who sets Madeline on the trail of the three missing paintings.

Penelope Kurkowski-Lorenz

She is a former French model who Sean fell in love with the moment he saw her. He followed her to Paris where he married her. Victim with their son of Beatriz Muñoz's revenge, from which she keeps physical after-effects, she is the only witness of Julian's murder.

KEYS TO READING

A MULTIPLE THRILLER

The literary genre of the thriller is characterised by omnipresent suspense, numerous twists and turns and tension. All these elements are present in this story, the outcome of which remains unpredictable until the end.

At the beginning of the story, *An Apartment in Faris is* presented as a classic romantic comedy: two characters who are at odds with each other are forced to live together. But very quickly, the novel takes or the character of a police investigation to find the three hypothetical last paintings that Sean Lorenz made before his death. While the discovery of the works closes the investigation led by Madeline and Gaspard, it leads to a new and unexpected enigma: the little Julian whom his mother Penelope claims to have seen murdered before her eyes, is still alive according to the painter. Is this a plausible hypothesis or the ramblings of a desperate, battered father? The doubt persists for a long time for our two heroes.

The investigation to find Julian also has many twists and turns. At first, Gaspard is sincerely convinced, as is Sean, that they will find the child alive since his body has never been discovered. However, the death of Adriano Sotomayor, the kidnapper, convinces Madeline and Gaspard that Julian is dead. Unexpectedly, evidence uncovered by examining Adriano's frequent purchases gives them hope that Sean and Penelope's son is alive. However, when they finally manage to locate him, the discovery of the lifeless body of Bianca, Adriano's mother who was locked up with the boy, makes them fear the worst before an unexpectedly happy ending.

A third plot in the form of a multi-stage cold case is added to the investigation into the disappearance of Sean and Penelope's son. The two investigators first question the true personality of Adriano Sotomayor. Then, they set about solving the case of the "Alder King" to understand what really happened to little Julian. These discoveries help explain the death of Reuben Sotomayor, Adriano's half-brother, the disappearance of their mother Bianca and the kidnapping and murder of several young children.

Solving these multiple riddles is an obligatory step for our characters in their investigation of Julian Lorenz, but it has the particularity of advancing the investigation while slowing it down, which helps to maintain the suspense.

Finally, the alternation of focus between Madeline and Gaspard is another device that maintains the suspense: it breaks the rhythm of the story and multiplies the twists and turns, since the discoveries are made sometimes by one and sometimes by the other.

AN INITIATION STORY

While *Un Appartement à Paris* has all the hallmarks of a thriller, it is also an initiation story for the two main characters, Madeline Greene and Gaspard Coutances.

Indeed, we observe a profound transformation of their personalities, associated with the discovery of new values: love and family for Gaspard, family for Madeline. This transformation will take place gradually through the investigation that the two heroes will carry out to try to find the last paintings of Sean Lorenz and, subsequently, his son, Julian.

"Without admitting it to themselves, Madeline and Gaspard both clung to the mad belief that these secrets would deliver them a truth, for, in searching for these paintings, it was also a part of themselves that they were tracking down." (p.178). At the beginning of the novel, Madeline attempts suicide after seeing her former partner with his baby boy, the child she would have loved to have with him. Since she survived thanks to her best friend's intervention at the last minute, her age and the lack of a serious relationship lead her to undertake an *in vitro* fertilisation process. Determined to rebuild her life – this is the reason for her stay in Paris – she dreams of a family, but does not envisage a man being part of it, because "her heart no longer had the strength to love" (p.141).

Misanthropic and technophobic, Gaspard has rejected any plans to start a family. Indeed, why would he voluntarily inflict on a child who did not ask to be born into such a world? The writer did not have a happy child-hood: his mother prevented him from seeing his father – whom he managed to meet with the help of the nanny – and the latter finally hanged himself after being arrested while fighting to recover his parental rights.

Although their joint investigation into the last three works of the painter Sean Lorenz has taught them to communicate with each other since their first stormy encounter in Paris, it is their departure for New York and the investigation into little Julian that really marks the first upheaval in the lives of the two protagonists.

A first step in the evolution of Gaspard's character is taken when he tries to hold Madeline back as she pre-pares to fly to Madrid, where she is to begin her *in vitro* fertilisation procedure. He, who does not want a child, is the first to be convinced that little Julian is alive and well, and he takes the initiative in this endeavour. This change is also expressed physically as Karen, his agent, perceives it. "You've shaved, you don't have your glasses anymore, you wear suits and you smell like lavender" (p. 300)

But the real shock, the point of no return, takes place in New York, at the very moment when Gaspard holds little Julian in his arms and Julian asks him if he is his father. After a brief hesitation, the playwright finally answers in the affirmative. And so, stuck in traffic on the way to the hospital, Gaspard tries again, sensing that he and Madeline have reached a pivotal point in their story: they can return little Julian to the authorities and go their separate ways, or they can form a family and give the battered boy a home.

This proposal from the writer causes a profound upheaval in the ex-policewoman: recognising her own fragility and finally accepting it, she opts for this family and couple life that she had decided to reject for fear of loving and suffering again.

This is the beginning of a new life for this trio.

Without knowing it, Julian was thus the factor of a profound transformation, slow or fast depending or the character, of Madeline and Gaspard, as told in the epilogue.

"For Madeline, for me, for you, the beginning of a new existence. A real rebirth" (p. 531).

THE IMPORTANCE OF THE ARTISTIC PROCESS

"Art is like a fire, it is born of what it burns. – Jean-Luc Godard (p. 181)

Art is omnipresent in this story, as is the artistic process, which, according to the elements presented by Musso, can only arise from suffering. The character of Sean Lorenz is presented as the archetypal tortured artist.

An unhappy childhood seems to be a common denominator between Sean and Gaspard. The former was never recognised by his father. He was expelled from school, fell into petty crime and joined a tagging group in his late teens, when he had a 'youthful appearance, but a face that was already troubled' (p.72). The second was prevented by his mother from seeing his father. Only with the complicity of his nanny did Gaspard manage to meet his father episodically, until he inadvertently mentions that they went to the cinema together. Unintentionally, he condemns his father to the loss of his parental rights and to suicide, after being arrested by the police when he wanted to fight to continue seeing his son.

This suffering feeds the productivity of Gaspard, who every year at Christmas time inflicts on himself a month of solitary writing in Paris, a city linked to his unhappy childhood where he was deprived of his father. This is what he himself describes as 'a technique of writing in a hostile environment' (p.27). Unlike Sean Lorenz, the playwright is aware of the impact of his unhappiness on his creation; he is realistic about his alcohol problem. Loneliness, dissatisfaction and sadness enable him to write, which his agent, Karen, understands very well: that is why she lets him lead this kind of life.

As for Sean, suffering is a constant friend. He finds inspiration in his tumultuous relationship with Penelope. She acts as his muse: he has painted twenty-one portraits of her, but not without endangering his sanity. The former model claims to be drained, describing her ex-husband's painting as a 'cannibal' that 'killed you in order to exist' (p.194). Sean's psychiatrist confirms this opinion: "The old principle of creative destruction.

To build a work like his, perhaps it was inevitable that Sean would destroy himself and others." (p. 169).

Moreover, Sean also applied this destruction to his own work. A perfectionist – or eternally dissatisfied – he did not hesitate to destroy all his work: "When he was not satisfied with a painting, Lorenz would burn it immediately. Between 1999 and 2013, he painted more than two thousand canvases, almost all of which he destroyed. Only about forty paintings escape his ferocious judgment." (p. 84).

This theory of the unhappy artist is confirmed by the birth of Sean's son. Having hoped and waited for this child for ten long years, the artist is overjoyed when Julian finally arrives, although this birth coincides with an artistic sterility that will last three years. Indeed, as the Gaspard agent said: "Happiness is nice to live with, but it's not very good for creation. Do you know any artists who are happy?" This artistic impediment to happiness also invades Gaspard, who decides to stop writing even though he has budding feelings for Madeline.

When his son disappears, the pain this time seems too strong to be sublimated into artistic creation: Lorenz stops his painting completely and falls back "into his old demons: drugs, alcohol, pills." (p. 89). It is only the mad hope that he will find his son alive after his near-death experiences that gives him the strength to paint again. The fragile but vivid hope, tinged with immense uncertainty, becomes the fertile ground for a new artistic period.

AVENUES FOR REFLECTION

A FEW QUESTIONS FOR FURTHER REFLECTION...

- "Paris is always a good idea." (p.25). How and to which characters can this quote from Audrey Hepburn be applied?

- "Mum, look, I'm flying." What role does this phrase play at the beginning and end of the novel?

- Musso's novel could be described as a "gigogne narrative". Explain why and the effects of this.

- Is Gaspard really the misanthrope we think he is? What about Madeline?

- How do you explain Madeline's reaction when Gaspard asks her if she wants a child to feel fulfilled and whole?

- The question of fatherhood is an important part of this story. What is its role?

- "I am deeply optimistic about nothing at all" (p.117). Which character(s) might also have uttered this sentence by Francis Bacon? Why or why not?

- Explain the role of the next four chapters: 'Gaspard', 'Penelope' (twice) and 'Bianca'? What do they contribute to the writing of the rest of the story?

TO GO FURTHER

REFERENCE EDITION

- MUSSO G., *Un Appartement à Paris*, Paris, Pocket, 2018.

Your opinion is important to us!
Leave a comment on the website of your online bookshop
and share your favourites on social networks!